Everyone Loves Fox + Chick!

★ "In the tradition of Frog and Toad and Elephant and Piggie."
—*School Library Journal*, starred review

★ "A perfect choice for those who . . . aren't quite ready for lengthier chapter books."
—*School Library Journal*, starred review

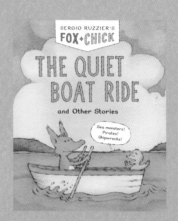

A Theodor Seuss Geisel
Honor Book

A School Library Journal Best
Children's Book of the Year

A New York Times Notable
Children's Book

A Junior Library Guild Selection

An NPR Best Book of the Year

An Amazon Best Book
of the Month

A Publishers Weekly Best
Book of the Year

A Texas Library Association
Little Maverick
Graphic Novel Selection

A School Library Journal Best
Children's Book of the Year

A Parents.com Best Summer
Reading Book for Kids

A Horn Book Fanfare Best
Book of the Year

A Today.com Best Gift & Toy
for 6-Year-Olds

To Sophie, Brian, Eddie, and Johnny.

ISBN 978-1-7972-0884-8

Library of Congress Cataloging-in-Publication Data:

Names: Ruzzier, Sergio, 1966- author, illustrator.
Title: The quiet boat ride and other stories / by Sergio Ruzzier.
Description: San Francisco, California : Chronicle Books LLC, [2019] |
Series: Fox + Chick ; book 2 | Summary: Fox enjoys quiet boat rides
and watching the sunrise, but Chick is noisy and hyperactive
and frequently disrupts their adventures—nevertheless
they remain friends and enjoy their time together.
Identifiers: LCCN 2018009424 | ISBN 9781452152899 (alk. paper)
Subjects: LCSH: Foxes—Juvenile fiction. | Chicks—Juvenile fiction. | Friendship—
Juvenile fiction. | Patience—Juvenile fiction. | Humorous stories. | CYAC: Foxes—Fiction. |
Chickens—Fiction. | Friendship—Fiction. | Patience—Fiction. | Humorous stories. |
LCGFT: Humorous fiction.
Classification: LCC PZ7.R9475 Qu 2019 | DDC [E]—dc23
LC record available at https://lccn.loc.gov/2018009424

Manufactured in China.

MIX
Paper from
responsible sources
FSC™ C008047
FSC
www.fsc.org

Design by Sara Gillingham Studio.
Paperback design by Riza Cruz.
Handlettering by Sergio Ruzzier.
The illustrations in this book were rendered in pen, ink, and watercolor.

10 9 8 7 6 5 4 3 2 1

Chronicle Books LLC
680 Second Street
San Francisco, California 94107
www.chroniclekids.com

SERGIO RUZZIER'S

FOX + CHICK

THE QUIET BOAT RIDE

and Other Stories

chronicle books · san francisco

CONTENTS

THE QUIET BOAT RIDE

WHAT ARE YOU DOING, FOX?

I'm going for a quiet boat ride.

5

Can I be the captain?

We don't need a captain, Chick.

Captain Chick! That sounds good.

What does a captain do, Fox?

A captain sits still and quiet.

I'm not the captain anymore, then.

Are there sea monsters down there?

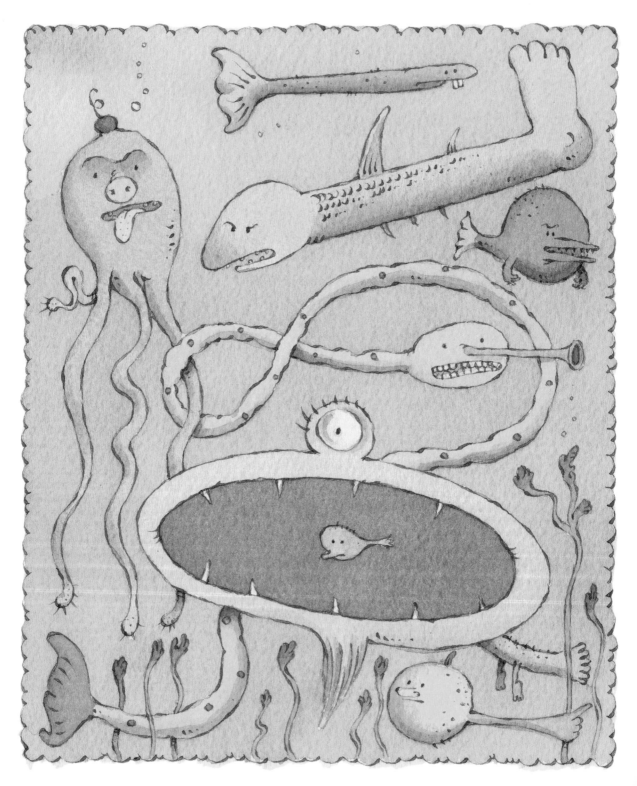

I am not fond of sea monsters.

Don't worry, Chick. This is a pond, not a sea.

Are there pirates in this pond?

I would hate to get shipwrecked.

Don't worry, Chick. We could swim to shore.

I don't know, Fox. This was supposed to be a quiet boat ride.

CHOCOLATE CAKE

I knew
this would
happen.

24

25

THE
SUNRISE

RIIIIING!

Where are you going, Fox?

To watch the sunrise from a hilltop.

But, it's so early!

That's when the sun rises, Chick.

What should I wear, Fox?

Chick, please hurry.

Should I take
an umbrella?

It's not
raining, and
if it was, we
wouldn't see
any sunrise.

Should I bring
a salami?

We'll eat
later, Chick.
Hurry!

We're going
to miss
the sunrise!

Should I take my hammer?

What do you need your hammer for?!

I can't find my hammer.

Chick,
let's go!

It was such
a nice hammer.

Where's this sunrise, Fox?

Also by Sergio Ruzzier

"Sweet, profound. Pays a sneaky
tribute to the power of words
and pictures."
—*The New York Times*

A Publishers Weekly
Best Book of the Year

A Parents' Choice Gold Award

A New York Times
Notable Children's Book

★ *School Library Journal*,
starred review

A School Library Journal
Best Children's Book of the Year

★ *Kirkus Reviews*,
starred review

A Huffington Post
Best Picture Book of the Year
Honorable Mention

★ *Publishers Weekly*,
starred review

Sergio Ruzzier is a 2011 Sendak Fellow
who has written and illustrated many
critically acclaimed children's books. Born
in Milan, Italy, he now divides his time
between Brooklyn, New York, and
the Apennine Mountains in Italy.